DISNEY·PIXAR

MONSTERS, INC.

SCREAM TEAM

Library of Congress Cataloging-in-Publication Data:
West, Cathy.
        Monsters, Inc., Scream team / adapted by Cathy West.
            p. cm.
        At head of title: Disney/Pixar.
        Summary: Monsters Mike and Sulley are terrorized by a human child and discover an evil plot at Monsters, Incorporated.
        ISBN 0-7364-1262-X
        [1. Monsters—Fiction.] I. Title: Scream team. II. Walt Disney Company. III. Pixar Animation Studios. IV. Monsters, Inc. (Motion Picture) V. Title.
PZ7.W5174 Mo 2001
[Fic]—dc21   2001031658

Printed in the United States of America
October 2001
10 9 8 7 6 5 4 3 2 1

www.randomhouse.com/kids/disney

DISNEY·PIXAR
MONSTERS, INC.
SCREAM TEAM

Adapted by Cathy West

Designed by Disney's Global Design Group

A STEPPING STONE BOOK™

Random House 🏫 New York

CHAPTER 1

It's midnight. The moon casts eerie shadows on an ordinary house, where an ordinary boy sleeps alone in his room.

Creeeeak...

The boy sits up and looks around. What is that? It sounds like the closet door opening! He stares into the darkness.

He sees nothing. So he snuggles back down into his bed.

Creeeeak...

*Something is creeping across the floor!
The boy shivers and peeks out from under
the covers.*

A long tentacle reaches for him!

*But no . . . it's only a shirtsleeve dangling
in the open closet.*

*The boy huddles under the covers as a
pair of evil eyes peer out from the darkness
under the bed.*

*Suddenly, the monster rises, his hulking
form blocking the moonlight, his arms
stretched back, ready to scare. He opens his
mouth wid. . . .*

The child opens his mouth and screams.

*The monster screams, too, and steps back
in fear. He slips on a ball, which shoots out
from under his foot, flies into the wall, and
hits him on the head. Still backing up, he
steps on a skateboard, falls, and lands on a
pile of jacks. As he hops around in pain, he*

knocks over a dresser, which lands on his foot.

The lights came on. The boy jerked to a stop. Then he flopped over in the bed like a doll.

The monster groaned. *I must have really messed up!* he thought.

"Simulation terminated!" said a computerized voice.

The boy in the bed wasn't real. The

bedroom wasn't real. It was all fake—like the set of a play. This was a training room at Monsters, Inc., where monsters learned how to scare kids.

Behind a desk, a tall, dragonlike monster named Ms. Flint shook her head. "Uh, Mr. Bile, can you tell me what you did wrong?"

"I fell down?" said Bile.

"Can anyone tell me what Mr. Bile did wrong? Anyone?" Ms. Flint asked the class of monsters seated in the training room. These monsters were all recruits,

newly hired at Monsters, Inc.

The monsters squirmed. Someone coughed.

"Let's take a look at the tape," Ms. Flint said with a sigh.

She punched a button, and a video of Bile filled a big screen.

"Ha! Right there! See?" Ms. Flint pointed at the door to the child's closet. "*The door*. You left it wide open."

"Oooh," the students murmured.

"And leaving a door open is the worst mistake any employee can make because . . . ?" Ms. Flint began.

"It could . . . let in a draft?" Bile guessed.

"It could let in a

child!" a voice boomed from the back of the room as a blue, crablike monster emerged from the shadows.

"Oh! Mr. Waternoose!" exclaimed Ms. Flint.

The students gasped.

Henry J. Waternoose was the CEO of Monsters, Inc., and everyone's boss.

"There is nothing more toxic or deadly than a human child. A single touch could kill you. Leave a door open, and a child could walk right into the monster world!" said Waternoose.

Terrified, one of the recruits jumped into the lap of the monster sitting next to him. "I won't go in a kid's room! You can't make me! Oh, no!" he moaned.

Disgusted, Waternoose pulled a yellow

canister from behind his back. "You're going in there because we need *this*!" he explained as he uncorked the can.

A scream split the air. The lights in the room surged and the computer monitors crackled. The recruits covered their ears. Waternoose corked the can.

"Our city is counting on you to collect

those children's screams," he said. "Without screams, we have no power."

The recruits gulped and shifted nervously in their seats.

Mr. Waternoose glanced around the room. He was worried. It was getting more and more difficult to find good Scarers. And lately, there had been an energy shortage.

So much had changed since his great-grandfather had started Monsters, Inc., many years ago. Human kids weren't so innocent anymore. Now that they had video games and television, they were a lot harder to scare.

Somehow he had to fix that.

James P. Sullivan, known to everyone as Sulley, and his roommate, Mike Wazowski, decided to walk to work because of the energy shortage in Monstropolis.

Sulley and Mike were best friends. They had been best friends since their first day of kindergarten, back when they were just little monsters.

They didn't look anything alike. Sulley

was huge. He was covered in blue-green fur with purple spots. Mike looked like a giant green pea with arms and legs and horns. He had one huge eyeball in the middle of his body. He was so short that he only came up to Sulley's belly button.

Sulley and Mike both worked at Monsters, Inc. Sulley was the best Scarer in the company. He even starred in their TV commercials. But he would never have

become the best Scarer without Mike. Mike was the best assistant in the business. They made a great team.

As the guys entered the building, they waved to Celia. She was a tall, slim purple monster with arms like an octopus. She had one baby blue eye and had snakes on her head instead of hair.

"Oh, Schmoopsie-Poo," Mike said, "I just got us into a little place called, um ... Harryhausen's."

The snakes on Celia's head wriggled in surprise. "But it's impossible to get a reservation there!" she cried.

Mike grinned. "Not for Googly Bear. I'll see you at 5:01, and not a minute later."

Then he and Sulley headed toward their workstation.

A huge, sluglike monster with a tuft of purple hair glared at Mike over her eyeglasses.

He tried to charm her, too. "Good morning, Roz, my succulent little garden snail. And who would we be scaring today?"

He reached for a pile of paperwork. But Roz's big wet hand slapped down on it first.

"Wazowski," she snarled. "You didn't file your paperwork last night."

"Oh, that darn paperwork," said Mike. "Wouldn't it be easier if it all just ... blew away?"

Roz leaned over her desk threateningly. "Don't let it happen again," she warned.

Mike moved away from Roz.

"Yes! Well, I'll try to be less careless," he muttered.

"I'm watching you, Wazowski," Roz replied. "Always ..."

Mike hurried onto the Scare Floor, a huge room bustling with activity. Above him, a voice on the intercom blared: "All Scare Floors are now active. Assistants, please report to your stations."

Sulley and Mike hurried to get ready.

Mike grabbed an empty yellow scream canister and loaded it into his door station. When Sulley scared a kid, the kid's scream would flow into the canister, where it was stored until it was needed for energy.

Next, Mike pulled a door card key from a folder. He took the card key, which had a picture of a human child on it, and slid it through a slot. Then he stood back and looked up as a door emerged from a vault. It slid into Mike and Sulley's station. All around them, doors descended from the vault and slid into place.

"Okay, people," called the floor manager. "Eastern Seaboard coming on line! We got Scarers coming out!"

From the shadows at the end of the hall emerged Sulley and the other Scarers, a frightening bunch of monsters in all shapes and colors. Each one had a special talent for scaring. Each monster was matched perfectly to the children he scared.

The Scarers prepared for the day's work. Lining up in front of their door stations, they cleaned their fangs and adjusted their eyeballs. They practiced their growls and roars.

Mike looked up at the scoreboard. It kept count of how many screams each monster collected. Sulley was in first place. But in second place was Randall Boggs, a mean monster who looked like a purple lizard and could blend into his surroundings like a chameleon.

"Hey," Sulley said to Randall, trying to be a good sport. "May the best monster win."

"I plan to," Randall said with a sneer.

The Scarers were ready.

Mike hit a button on his keypad, and the

red light above his door flashed on.

A horn sounded. The Scarers shot through their doors.

Seconds later...

"AGGHHHHH!"

Screams could be heard through all the doors.

Mike watched gleefully as his pal Sulley scared kid after kid, filling scream canisters faster than any other Scarer.

Soon, Sulley popped out of one of the doors. He glanced at the tally board. His numbers were climbing. He was in the lead.

"Oh, I'm feeling good today, Mikey," Sulley said.

"Atta boy!" Mike shouted. "Another door coming right up!"

Sulley ran through door after door. His scream canisters filled up. They tumbled into a holder. His numbers climbed.

But so did Randall's.

Suddenly, loud rock music filled the air. A door flew open, and a huge monster stumbled out. *"Ahhhh!"* he cried as he slammed the door.

"What happened?" his assistant asked.

"The kid almost touched me!" the monster cried. "She got *this* close to me!"

"She wasn't scared of you?" The assistant looked down at his paperwork. "She was only six!"

The assistant gave a loud whistle. "Hey, we've got a dead door over here!"

Two workers came running, wheeling a portable door shredder between them. They taped a big yellow X across the door.

The workers lowered the door into one end of the shredder. *Bzzzz!* Wooden chips spewed out the other end.

Mr. Waternoose, who had stopped by to see how things were going, shook his head as he watched. Shredding a child's door meant that the child could no longer be scared. One more source of scream energy was gone.

"We've lost fifty-eight doors this week, sir," Jerry, the floor manager, said.

Waternoose sighed. "Kids these days. They just don't get scared like they used to."

Just then, Randall rushed out of his door. His assistant, Fungus, pointed up at the tally board.

Randall grinned as he watched his name move to first place. Sulley moved down to second.

Celia announced the news over the loud-speaker. "Attention! We have a new scare leader: Randall Boggs."

Some of the monsters cheered.

But suddenly several screams filled the air. Mike hurried to load a new scream canister. Then that one filled up, too. Before he was finished, fifteen canisters had been filled with screams. Wow! His partner Sulley was the best!

At last the door swung open. The big blue monster strolled out and cracked his knuckles.

"Slumber party," Sulley said with a chuckle.

The numbers on the tally board spun. Sulley was back in first place.

"That was awesome!" someone shouted. "You're going to the hall of fame for sure!"

"Well, James, that was an impressive display," said Mr. Waternoose.

"Oh, just doing my job, Mr. Waternoose." Sulley smiled modestly. "Of course, I did learn from the best."

Waternoose laughed and slapped Sulley on the back.

Randall watched, his heart twisting with jealousy. "If I don't see a new door in my station in five seconds," he hissed at

Fungus, "I will personally put you through the shredder!"

Nearby, a monster named George Sanderson danced out of his door. He looked really happy.

"Keep the doors coming," he said to his assistant, Charlie. "I'm on a roll today!"

Charlie nodded. But then his eyes grew wide with horror.

"We have a twenty-three nineteen!"

he shouted as he pointed at George.

"Red alert! Red alert!" Sirens wailed. Everyone on the Scare Floor froze.

George looked around. Somebody was in trouble. But who?

A security camera pointed at George. His picture filled a huge TV screen as a computerized voice announced, "George Sanderson, please remain motionless. Prepare for decontamination."

Everyone gasped at what they saw.

A child's sock was stuck to George's furry back!

CHAPTER 3

"Get it off! Get it off!" George screamed.

Everyone scattered.

Agents from the CDA—the Child Detection Agency—swarmed onto the floor.

They tackled George to the ground.

One agent held out some tongs. Very, very carefully, he picked off the sock. Then he dropped the sock under a high-tech metal dome. Everyone stepped back.

Someone pushed a button. There was an explosion. Lights flashed. Smoke filled the air.

The agent lifted up the dome. The sock had been totally destroyed.

But agents vacuumed up the charred remains just to be sure.

"Hey, thanks, guys," George said.

The agents rushed George again,

surrounding him with a portable shower curtain. An electric razor buzzed and fur flew. George was getting a head-to-toe shave!

When the buzzing stopped, a powerful blast of hot cleaner streamed down on the poor monster. George let out a bloodcurdling scream.

At last, they led George away.

"Okay, people, take a break!" the floor manager called out. "We gotta shut down for a half hour and reset the system."

Mr. Waternoose groaned. "What else can go wrong?" he muttered.

At last, the long workday came to an end. Mike and Sulley walked to the lobby.

"I've never seen anything like you today!" Mike exclaimed. "You were on a roll, my man!"

Sulley nodded. He wasn't one to brag. But he loved what he did, and he was proud of his hard work. Scaring kids was an important job. "Another day like this and that scare record's in the bag," Sulley said.

"That's right, baby!" said Mike. "What's on your agenda for tonight?"

"I'm going to head home and work out some more," said Sulley.

"Again? You know, there's more to life than scaring," said Mike. "What a night of romance I've got ahead of me!"

"Hello, Wazowski." Roz slid up to him. "Fun-filled evening planned for tonight?"

Mike sputtered as if a bucket of cold water had been dropped on his head. "Well, as a matter of fact—"

"And I'm sure you filed your paperwork correctly," Roz added.

Mike gasped and turned to Sulley. "Oh, no. My scare reports!" he whispered. "I left them on my desk! If I'm not at the restaurant in five minutes, they're gonna give my table away. What am I going to tell—"

"Googly Bear!" Celia slipped an arm through his. "Want to get going?"

"Oh . . . do I ever . . . ," Mike sputtered. He quickly tried to think up an excuse. "It's just that . . . uh—"

Sulley came to his friend's rescue. "It's just that *I* forgot about some paperwork I was supposed to file," Sulley said, covering for his buddy. "Mike was reminding me."

"Okay, let's go then," said Celia. She turned and began to walk away. Mike followed her. Sulley headed back to their station to find Mike's paperwork.

Back on the Scare Floor, everything was quiet.

Then Sulley saw it—a single door was still positioned and active in its station. *That's weird,* he thought. All the doors

were supposed to be put away in the vault each night.

Puzzled, Sulley walked over and opened the door. "Hello? Hey. *Psst.* Is anybody scaring in here?" he called out softly.

There was no answer.

Sulley stepped back and shut the door. He wasn't sure what to do.

Suddenly, he felt something strange.

His tail was being lifted up and dropped on the floor with a thump.

He turned around and gasped!

It was *the* most terrifying thing he had ever seen.

A human child—at Monsters, Inc.!

CHAPTER 4

The little girl smiled at Sulley.

Sulley screamed and fell backward with a crash.

He grabbed the tongs the CDA agent had left. Trying hard not to squish the girl, he used the tongs to pick her up. He ran to the open door and placed her inside. Then he slammed the door and turned around. *Whew! That was close,* thought Sulley.

Then he heard a giggle. She was right

behind him! Sulley screamed again. *How did she get out?*

Sulley gulped. He had to be brave! He made himself pick up the little girl with his bare hands. He opened the door, ran into her room, dropped her on the bed, and turned to run.

But on his way out, he ran into a mobile hanging from the ceiling. Startled, Sulley stepped back—right into a laundry basket. He fell down and slid out of the room, completely covered in clothing.

Sulley gasped. This was too awful to be true. He was covered with horrible things. *Human* things! *Kid* things!

Out on the Scare Floor, he heard footsteps. *Someone's coming!* he thought.

He stumbled into the men's locker room to hide. He tried to flush the human things down the toilet, but it spewed everything back out. So he stuffed them all into a locker.

Calm down, Sulley thought. *Everything's okay. It's all over.*

Then he felt a yank on one of his horns. It wasn't over! The human child was still there—and she was on his back!

He brushed her off and ran. But the tiny creature followed him. He cowered on a bench. What was she going to do?

She looked up at him and babbled. Then she smiled. "Kitty!" she said with delight.

Sulley didn't know what to do. Then he spotted a Monsters, Inc., duffel bag. He scooped the girl into the bag and ran out of the locker room.

Sulley headed straight for the Scare Floor. He had to put the kid back before anyone found out what had happened.

But as he approached her door, he

heard the knob rattle. In a panic, Sulley dove behind the door.

Seconds later, the door opened and Randall emerged! He hit a button that made the door rise up and return to the vault. He left without seeing Sulley trying to hide.

As soon as Randall was out of sight, Sulley took off with the bag with the kid in it. He had to find Mike! Together, he and his buddy would figure out what to do.

CHAPTER 5

Mike and Celia gazed into each other's eye at Harryhausen's, the hottest sushi restaurant in Monstropolis.

"Oof!" said Celia as Sulley suddenly squished into the booth with them.

"Sulley!" Mike whispered. "Get outta here. You're ruining everything!"

"I went back to get your paperwork," Sulley whispered back. "And there was a door. Randall was in it."

Mike gasped. "That cheater! He's trying to boost his numbers!"

"There's something else." Sulley nodded toward the bag under the table. "Ooklay in the agbay."

Mike frowned. "What?"

"Look in the bag!" Sulley answered.

Mike looked under the table. "What bag?" he asked.

Sulley looked down. The bag was gone!

A few tables over, a monster couple was celebrating their anniversary. They smiled as a photographer aimed his camera at them.

Suddenly, the couple's happy smiles froze. Something horrifying appeared over the photographer's shoulder. . . .

"Boo!" said the little girl, giggling gleefully.

"Aaaahhh!" the photographer screamed. "A kid!"

One of the sushi chefs picked up the phone and screamed into it: "There's a kid here! A *human* kid!"

Monsters were screaming and panicking and running for the door. Sulley tried to reach for the girl, but she dashed away, babbling happily.

Mike saw a large take-out box. He grabbed it and scooped the little girl into the box, being careful not to touch her. Then Sulley shut the lid.

"Come on!" yelled Sulley.

As they ran out of the restaurant, CDA agents arrived.

"We have an eight thirty-five in progress, please advise," said one of the agents.

"Stand clear!" another boomed.

"Michael! Michael!" Celia called above the commotion.

Mike spun around.

"Oh, Celia!" he said.

A CDA agent stepped in front of Celia.

"Come with us, please," he said, pushing Celia.

"Stop pushing!" said Celia.

Mike reached for Celia. "Hey! Get your hands off my Schmoopsie-Poo!" he yelled. But Sulley was tugging at him, and he knew he had to go with his friend.

Together, they raced down an alley.

"Well," said Mike. "I don't think that date could have gone any worse!"

With a huge *BOOM,* the sushi restaurant exploded into smithereens behind them.

Back at home, Sulley and Mike cowered behind a chair. They were dressed in protective gear to keep safe as the toxic toddler happily explored their apartment.

Helicopters whirred overhead. On the television set, a worried newscaster reported: "If witnesses are to be believed, there has been a child security breach for the first time in monster history."

"We can neither confirm nor deny the presence of a human child here tonight," said a CDA agent being interviewed at the restaurant.

"Well, a kid flew right over me and blasted a car with its laser vision!" exclaimed a monster on the scene.

"I tried to run from it, but it picked me up with its mind powers and shook me like a doll!" added another monster.

Meanwhile, Mike held out a can of disinfectant spray like a weapon. "As long as *that* doesn't come near us, we're going to be okay."

The little girl popped up and sneezed on his arm. Mike screamed.

Sulley noticed that the girl was pointing

at something. He glanced up. A teddy bear with one eye sat on the mantel. "Oh, you like this?" He tossed it over her head. "Fetch."

"Hey!" Mike exclaimed, grabbing the bear. "No one touches little Mikey."

The little girl's eyes filled with tears. She

opened her mouth and screamed.

Bzzt! Her scream made all the lights in the apartment flare! Outside the building, circling helicopters turned and headed in the direction of the light surge.

Seeing this through the window, Mike dropped the bear and ran to pull down the shade. Sulley picked up the bear and offered it to the little girl. But she wouldn't stop screaming. Desperate, Sulley began to dance with the bear, trying to make the kid calm down. "Oh, he's a happy bear, and he's not crying, and neither should you or we'll be in trouble, 'cause they're gonna find us. . . ."

"Sulley! The bear! Give it the—" As he rushed toward Sulley, reaching for the bear, Mike tripped on a lamp and flew across the room, tumbling into a garbage can. The garbage can banged against a shelf, sending a stack of books straight into Mike's open mouth. Mike looked up just in time to see a stereo speaker land on his head.

The little girl laughed. A great big laugh.

The lights flared again. But not just the ones in their apartment—all the lights in the whole building flared!

Finally, the girl's laugh faded. The lights went back to normal.

"What was that?" asked Sulley.

"I have no idea," said Mike. "But it would be really great if it didn't do it again."

The girl giggled.

Sulley put his finger to his lips. "Shhh."

The girl seemed to understand. She held her finger to her lips, too, and smiled cutely.

She understood him, and she was

starting to like her two new friends.

"How could I do this?" Sulley groaned. "This could destroy the company."

The little girl sat on the floor, drawing pictures with crayons.

"The company?" Mike exclaimed. "Who cares about the company? What about *us*? That thing is a killing machine!"

Sulley looked at the little girl as she colored happily. She didn't look like a killing machine. But they couldn't take any chances.

"Mike, I think she's getting tired," Sulley said.

The little girl yawned and held up the drawing she had made.

It was a nice picture. A happy picture. A picture of Sulley and the little girl.

Sulley made a trail of cereal on the

floor. The little girl followed it into Sulley's bedroom, picking up the pieces and eating them one at a time.

Then Sulley laid out some newspaper on the floor. He poured a pile of cereal in the middle. "Okay, I'm making a nice little area for you to—"

He looked up. The kid had curled up in his bed. "No, hey! That's *my* bed. You're gonna get your germs all over it!"

But she had already snuggled under the covers. And she looked so, well . . . cute.

"Ah, fine," Sulley grumbled. "My chair's more comfortable, anyway."

He started to leave. But then the little girl called out.

She was pointing at the closet door.

"It's just a closet," Sulley said. "Will you go to sleep?"

The little girl held up another drawing.

A drawing of a scary purple monster.

"Hey, that looks like Randall," Sulley said. Then he understood. "Randall's your monster."

He crossed to the closet and opened it. "No monster in here."

The little girl pulled the covers over her head as if she was sure there would be a monster in the closet.

"Okay, how about I sit here until you fall asleep?" Sulley said, wanting to comfort her. He pulled a cinder block in front of the closet and sat down.

The little girl smiled. Seconds later, she was fast asleep.

Sulley stared down at the child. He'd never really seen a human kid this close up. Well, not one that wasn't screaming its head off.

She was a cute little thing.

Harmless-looking, really.

James P. Sullivan was one of the best Scarers in the history of Monsters, Inc. He loved his job. Producing screams for energy was an important job. He was a good monster.

So why did he suddenly feel so *bad*?

CHAPTER 6

Sulley walked into the living room, deep in thought.

"Hey, Mike. This might sound crazy," he said, "but I don't think that kid is dangerous."

Mike stared at his friend. "Really? Well, in that case, let's keep it. I always wanted a pet—*that could kill me!*"

"Now look," Sulley said. "What if we just put her back in her door?"

"What?" Mike exclaimed.

"Think about it. If we send her back, it's like it never happened. Everything goes back to normal," Sulley said.

Mike couldn't believe what he was hearing. Sulley was his hero. Was he getting soft on . . . humans?

"Sulley! That is a *horrible* idea!" Mike exclaimed. "What are we gonna do? March right out into public with that thing? Then I guess we just waltz right up to the factory, right?"

"I can't believe we are waltzing right up to the factory," Mike said early the next morning.

Sulley was carrying the little girl in his arms. But he'd dressed her up in a monster costume. As long as no one looked too closely, she looked like any other monster child. She seemed happy, as if she thought it was a big game.

Sulley pulled the girl's hood down over her face. "Don't panic. We can do this," he said to his buddy.

But as soon as they got into the building, Mike knew they'd made a mistake.

Monsters filled the hallways. And there were CDA agents everywhere!

The friends managed to sneak the girl into the men's locker room.

"Okay," Mike said. "All we have to do is get rid of that *thing*. So wait here while I get its card key."

"But she can't stay here," Sulley said, horrified. "This is the *men's* room."

Mike rolled his eye. "That is the weirdest thing you have ever said. It's fine! Look, it loves it here. It's dancing with joy!"

And with that, he stomped out the door.

The little girl babbled at Sulley.

Sulley smiled at her. "Ha, ha. That's a cute little dance you've got. It almost looks like you got to—oh!" he said, finally understanding.

The kid obviously needed to go to the bathroom. Sulley opened a stall door. Then he stood guard in case any monsters came in.

But when she hadn't come out after a while, he started to get worried. He peeked in the stall. It was empty!

Then he heard her giggle. So she wanted to play hide-and-seek, huh? He tiptoed two doors down. "Gotcha!" he said, opening the door.

But she wasn't there!

"Boo!" she cried from behind him.

Sulley laughed. "Hey, you're good!"

A few minutes later, Mike came back.

He didn't have the card key. Roz wouldn't give it to him because he—or rather, Sulley—had never turned in his paperwork from the night before.

He'd just have to fake it somehow.

Mike found Sulley on his hands and knees on the bathroom floor. "What are you doing?" he demanded.

Sulley looked embarrassed. "Uh, I'm looking for the kid."

"You lost it?" Mike exclaimed.

"No, no . . . ," said Sulley sheepishly.

Suddenly, the little girl ran in and grabbed Sulley's arm. But she wasn't giggling anymore.

"What's the matter?" Sulley asked.

The girl pointed.

Randall and Fungus were coming in the door! Sulley, Mike, and the girl ducked into a stall to hide.

"Randall!" Fungus whispered. "It's on the front page! The child you were after— it may have survived the blast in the restaurant!"

"You just get the machine up and running. I'll take care of the kid," Randall said. "And when I find whoever let it out . . . they're dead!"

The door banged shut.

Mike and Sulley stared at each other. This wasn't good at all.

CHAPTER 7

"This is bad," Mike said as they quietly slipped into the hall. "This is so very bad."

"Don't panic," Sulley said. "All we have to do is call her door down and send her home. You got her card key, right?"

"Of *course* I have her card key," Mike fibbed.

As they passed some workers, Mike sneaked a card key out of one of their folders.

He joined Sulley at their station. Then he slid the card key into the card slot and waited nervously.

So what if it isn't her exact *card key?* Mike thought. *It doesn't matter which door we shove her through, right? As long as we get rid of her.*

"Take care of yourself," Sulley told the little girl.

The door banged into position. Sulley stared at it. "That's not her door."

"Of course it's her door!" Mike snapped.

Sulley shook his head. "No. Her door was white. And it had flowers on it."

"It must have been dark last night. . . ." Mike insisted impatiently. "Because this is its door."

He yanked it open. Yodeling poured out. It was obviously not Boo's door. "Hear that? Sounds like fun in there.

Okay, send me a postcard, kid. Mike Wazowski, care of twenty-two Mike Wazowski 'You Got Your Life Back' Lane."

"Mike Wazowski!" the girl exclaimed.

But she didn't move. So Mike picked up a pencil. "Come on. See the stick? Go fetch." He threw it through the door.

A big blue hand shot out and slammed the door.

"Mike," Sulley insisted. "This *isn't* Boo's door."

"Boo?" Mike looked surprised. "What's 'Boo'?"

Sulley looked kind of embarrassed. "That's what I decided to call her. Is there a problem?"

"Sulley! You're not supposed to name it!" Mike shrieked. "Once you name it, you start getting attached to it! Now put that thing back where it came from, or so help me—"

He pointed at Boo. Only... she wasn't there.

"Where'd it go?" Mike exclaimed.

"Boo!" Sulley called out.

"I don't believe it!" Mike shrieked. But then he stopped. And smiled. "Wait a minute. This is perfect! Ha, ha—she's gone!"

Sulley scanned the room, searching for Boo. Then he took off across the room. Mike grabbed onto his friend's tail, trying to slow him down.

"Sulley, please don't blow this," Mike begged. "Somebody else will find the kid. It'll be their problem. Not ours."

Suddenly, Sulley spotted Boo and ran after her. Mike started to chase him. But then he heard:

"Michael Wazowski!" It was Celia. She looked awfully mad. The snakes on her head hissed angrily at him. "Last night was one of the worst nights of my entire life! I thought you cared about me!"

"Honey, please, Schmoopsie, I thought you liked sushi," Mike said.

"Sushi?" she exclaimed. "You think this is about *sushi*?"

Nearby, Randall hid behind a newspaper. He pretended to be reading. But he was listening to Mike and Celia argue.

So... Mike Wazowski was in the sushi restaurant, Randall thought. *The one*

where the human kid was spotted.

Soon Celia stomped off. Mike started to follow. But Randall blocked his path. "Where's the kid?" he snarled.

"Kid?" Mike gulped. "What kid?"

"It's here in the factory. Isn't it?" Randall said.

"You're not pinning this on me!" Mike said angrily. "It never would have gotten out if you hadn't been cheating last night!"

"Cheating! I—" Randall's eyes darted

back and forth. So Mike thought this was all about Randall's competition with Sulley. *Good*, Randall thought. *Let him think that.*

"Okay, I think I know how to make this all go away," said Randall. "In five minutes everyone goes to lunch, which means the Scare Floor will be empty. You have until then to put the kid back. Get the picture?"

Mike nodded. He decided he was going to have to trust Randall. But he wished Sulley were there.

CHAPTER 8

Sulley finally spotted Boo at the end of a hallway. She was reaching for something in a garbage can.

"Boo!" Sulley said under his breath, relieved.

Boo fell into the garbage can.

Sulley gasped.

At that moment, two workers grabbed the can and began to wheel it away. Sulley was about to call out to them when a voice bellowed, "Hey, you! Halt!" It was a CDA agent, and he was talking to Sulley.

Sulley froze as two CDA agents approached him.

"You're the one," said one of the agents.

"Uh..." Sulley panicked and couldn't think of anything to say.

"The one from the commercial!" said the agent.

"Affirmative, that's him," said the other agent.

"Can we get an autograph?" asked the first agent.

"Oh! Oh, sure... no problem," said Sulley nervously.

"If you could make that out to Bethany, my daughter..."

"Ah, yes!" said Sulley. "Let's see....From your scary friend...best wishes..."

Sulley handed the agent his autograph.

"Uh, see you guys later. Take it easy!" he said.

"Thanks a lot," said the CDA agent.

As soon as the agents were out of sight, Sulley swiftly turned around—just in time to see the workers lift the garbage can and dump the garbage down a chute!

Sulley raced to the basement. All the trash went there, and a compactor squashed it into tiny cubes.

He had to find Boo fast! This was terrible!

He ran into the compactor room. But it was too late.

The compactor had gobbled everything up!

CHAPTER 9

"Sulley!" Mike shouted. "I got us a way out of this mess! But we gotta hurry. Where is it?"

Suddenly, he noticed that Sulley was upset. And he was holding something. Something strange.

Sulley sniffled and held it up for Mike to see.

Mike scowled. "Sull, that's a cube of garbage," he said. Then he saw an eye stalk from Boo's monster costume sticking out. "Uh-oh."

"I can still hear her little voice," Sulley said sadly.

"Mike Wazowski!"

Mike looked puzzled. "Hey! *I* can hear her, too."

The two monsters looked around. A monster day-care teacher led a line of preschool mini-monsters down the hall to the bathroom.

At the end of the line was Boo—missing one eye stalk from her costume.

"Mike Wazowski!" she shouted.

Then she raised her arms in the air. "Kitty!"

"Boo!" Sulley picked her up and spun her around. He gave her a big hug. What a relief!

"Boo! Oh, you're all right! I was so

worried!" Sulley said happily. "Don't you ever run away from me again, young lady! Oh, but I'm *soooo* glad you're safe."

The day-care teacher smiled. "My, what an affectionate father," she said.

I think I'm gonna be sick! Mike thought. *We've got to get rid of that thing before Sulley completely loses his mind!*

"Okay," Mike said. "That's enough."

"I still don't understand," Sulley said. "You've got Boo's door?"

"I'll explain later," Mike replied. "Run!"

As they ran, Mike muttered, "Oh, please be there, please be there."

At last, they got to the Scare Floor. It was dark and empty. Everyone was at lunch.

Mike grinned when he saw Boo's door in the station. "There it is! Just like Randall said."

Sulley looked at the white door with the pink flowers and sighed. He knew he had to send Boo home. He knew she couldn't stay in Monstropolis. But something didn't feel right.

"One, two, three, four—get the kid back through the door," Mike said urgently. "We're gonna get our lives back. The nightmare is over."

Sulley knew Mike was right. This was their big chance to get Boo home. He knelt down and said goodbye to her. He wasn't ever going to see his little human friend again—but at least it would be the end of their troubles.

Then again, Sulley thought, *there's always more trouble when Randall is involved. I bet he's up to no good.*

Sulley was right. Randall *was* up to no good.

When Sulley refused to let Boo enter the room, Mike dashed in to prove it was safe—only to be captured in a box that popped up from the bed. Randall had set a trap to catch Boo! He rushed in, picked up the box, and took off down the hall.

Sulley and Boo ran after Randall, trying

to save their friend. They followed him to the basement of Monsters, Inc., where he turned a corner—and disappeared!

Randall brought the box to his secret lab. When he opened it and found Mike instead of Boo, he was furious, but he went on with his plan. He strapped Mike

to a horrible machine called a scream extractor. It was designed to suck all the scream out of a child. Randall wanted to kidnap children like Boo to test his machine on them. If the scream extractor worked, Randall could capture more scream power than any other worker at Monsters, Inc.

Luckily, just as Randall was turning on the machine, Boo found the hidden entrance to his lab. Sulley ran in to free Mike, and then he, Mike, and Boo made a quick getaway.

With no one else to turn to, they went to Waternoose for help. But Waternoose was part of Randall's evil plan! He wanted kids' screams to stop the power shortage and save Monsters, Inc. He grabbed Boo and banished Mike and Sulley to a frozen wasteland in the human world.

Sulley was determined to save Boo. He found a village, went through a closet door, and made it back to Monsters, Inc.,

just in time to save Boo from Randall and his scream extractor. And with Mike's help, Sulley sent Randall through a door and shredded it, banishing him to the human world forever.

Mike and Sulley turned Waternoose in to the CDA for plotting to kidnap children. When they did, they found out that Roz was the head of the whole agency. She was CDA agent Number One!

After a tearful goodbye, Boo was sent back through her flower-covered door. Then her door was shredded, too, so no one from the monster world could enter it again.

Sulley saved Monsters, Inc., with the secret he had discovered through Boo: children's laughter produces more power than their screams. This discovery put an end to Sulley and Mike's days as the best Scream Team ever. The Scare Floors became Laugh Floors. Sulley became the president of Monsters, Inc., with Mike as his top Laugh Collector. Monstropolis once again had more than enough energy for every monster in the city.

Sulley was happy that he had saved

Monsters, Inc., but he missed Boo. Then one day Mike surprised Sulley—he had saved the shredded pieces of Boo's door and put them back together! Now Sulley could visit Boo whenever he wanted. And Boo was always happy to see her big blue "Kitty."